SIX COMPANIONS FIND THEIR FORTUNE

A Tale by the Brothers Grimm illustrated by Lilo Fromm

Translated by Katya Sheppard

Doubleday & Company, Inc.

Garden City, New York

Library of Congress Catalog Card Number 79-127216
© 1969 Verlag Heinrich Ellermann, Munich
English text © 1969, Macdonald & Co. (Publishers) Ltd.
Printed in Germany

There was once a man who was good at many things. He served as a soldier, bravely and well. But when the war was over, all he got was threepence.

"That's not good enough," he said. "You wait. If I can find the right people to help me, I'll make the king give me all his treasure one day."

Full of anger he walked into a wood. There he saw a fellow who had pulled six trees out of the ground just like that. "Will you be my servant and go with me?" he asked.

"Yes," said Strong, "but let me take this little bundle of sticks home to my mother first."

Strong wrapped another tree round his bundle, slung it over his shoulder and carried it off. Then he came back to his new master, who said:

"We should make our way in the world, the two of us together."

When they had gone a little way they met a hunter, who was down on one knee and aiming his gun.

"What are you going to shoot?" asked the master.

"I mean to shoot a fly sitting on the branch of an oak tree, two miles off."

"Come with me, Hunter," the man said. "We should make our way in the world, the three of us together."

The hunter was willing, and went with him.

They came to seven windmills whose sails were spinning round, though there was not a breath of wind and not a leaf stirring. The man said: "I don't know what is driving these windmills, with never a breeze stirring," and walked on with his servants.

When they had gone two miles they saw someone sitting up a tree, holding one nostril shut and blowing out of the other.

"What on earth are you doing up there?" asked the man.

"There are seven windmills two miles away. Look: I'm blowing to make them work."

"Come with me, Blow," said the man; "we should make our way in the world, the four of us together."

So Blow climbed down and went with them.

After a while they saw a fellow standing on one leg; he had taken off the other and put it beside him.

"You look very comfortable, resting on one leg like that," said the man.

"I am a runner, and I have unstrapped one leg so that I don't run too fast; if I run on both legs I am speedier than any bird."

"Come with me, Speed! We should make our way in the world, the five of us together."

Before long they met a man whose hat was stuck right over one ear. "That looks very odd," the master said to him. "It makes you look a simpleton, wearing your hat all to one side like that."

"I have to," said the other; "if I were to put my hat on straight it would start a terrible frost, and all the birds in the sky would freeze and fall dead to the ground."

"Come with me, Frost," said the man. "We should make our way in the world, the six of us together."

Now one day the six of them came to a town where the king had made it known that whoever ran a race against his daughter and won would become her husband, but whoever lost would lose his head also.

So the master presented himself, but said: "I would like my servant to run in my stead."

"Then his life too—both your heads—will have to be at stake," replied the king.

When this had been agreed, the master buckled on Speed's other leg and said to him: "Now be swift and help us to win!"

It was decided that the first to bring back water from a distant well would be the winner. Speed and the king's daughter were each given a pitcher and the race began.

In an instant, Speed had disappeared out of sight —it was as if the wind had whistled past. He got to the well in no time, filled his pitcher with water and turned back again.

But half-way home Speed was overcome with tiredness. He lay down with his pitcher beside him and went to sleep—though he used a horse's skull lying on the ground as a pillow, so that he would be uncomfortable and wake up again soon.

The king's daughter could run as fast as any ordinary human being. She too reached the well and started running back with her pitcher full of water. When she saw Speed lying asleep she was glad and said: "Now the enemy is in my hands." She emptied his pitcher and raced on.

It seemed that all was lost, but luckily Hunter had been watching up at the castle with his sharp eyes, and had seen everything.

"The king's daughter is not going to get the better of us," he said. So he loaded his gun and most skilfully shot the horse's skull from under Speed's head without harming him.

Speed woke up, jumped to his feet and saw his empty pitcher and the king's daughter, way, way ahead of him. But he did not lose heart. He raced back to the well with his pitcher, filled it up again— and got back to the start ten minutes before the king's daughter.

"Here we are," he said. "I really got up speed this time. What I did before can scarcely be called running!"

But it grieved the king, and his daughter even more, that she was to be carried off by a common ex-soldier. They took counsel together on how to get rid of him and his companions.

"I have found a way," the king said at last. "Do not fear. They shall never reach their homes again." And to them he said: "Now you shall eat, drink and be merry!"

He led them to a room which had an iron floor, iron doors and iron bars across the windows, and in it a table spread with the most delicious food.

"Go in," said the king, "and enjoy yourselves!"

And when they had gone inside, the doors were locked and bolted on them.

Now the king sent for his cook and ordered him to light a fire beneath the room and keep it burning till the iron was red-hot. The cook did so, and as the fire burned up, the six companions, sitting at the table, began to feel very warm. They thought it was because of the food, but as it grew hotter and hotter they tried to get out; and when they found the doors and windows were bolted, they realized that the king meant mischief and wanted to stifle them.

But Frost said: "He shall not succeed: *I'll* cause a frost that will shame the fire and make it creep away!" And he put his hat on straight.

At once it grew so bitterly cold that the heat simply vanished and the very food froze on their plates.

After an hour or two the king felt sure they must have perished in the heat, so he had the doors unlocked in order to see for himself. But as they swung open all six of them stood there together, hale and hearty. They would be pleased to come out and get warm, they said; the very food had frozen on their plates with the bitter chill inside!

Raging with fury, the king went down to scold his cook: "Why did you not do as I ordered?"

"There's plenty of heat here—you can see for yourself," the cook replied.

When the king saw the huge fire burning under the iron chamber, he knew that he could not get the better of the six companions like that.

Then the king tried another way to rid himself of his unwelcome guests. He called the master to him and said: "If you will renounce your right to my daughter's hand, you shall have as much gold as you want."

"Very well, Sire," said the master; "give me as much as my servant can carry and I will not demand your daughter." The king being satisfied, he went on: "I will come back in a fortnight to collect the gold."

Then he got together all the tailors in the kingdom and made them sit for fourteen days and sew a sack. When it was finished it was up to Strong to hoist it on his shoulder and carry it to the king.

"Who is this gigantic fellow carrying that bale of stuff the size of a house?" wondered the king. He was quite shaken. "Think of the gold *he* could carry off!" He had a ton of gold brought; it needed sixteen of his toughest men to carry it. But Strong picked it up with one hand, put it in the sack and said: "Hurry, bring me some more—this hardly covers the bottom!"

Bit by bit the king caused the whole of his treasure to be brought out. Strong pushed it all into the sack, which was still less than half full.

"More, more," he cried. "These few crumbs haven't filled it."

Seven thousand carts laden with gold had to be got together from all over the kingdom: Strong pushed every one into his sack—oxen and all. But there was still plenty of room.

At last Strong said: "Well, we've wasted enough time now, so tie up the sack, although it is not full." Then he hoisted it up on his back and went off with his companions.

It enraged the king to see one man carrying off the entire riches of his country! He got his horsemen to chase the six companions, with orders to remove the sack from Strong. Two regiments soon caught up with them, calling out: "You are prisoners! Put down the sack full of gold or you'll all be hacked to pieces!"

"What's that?" said Blow; "us — prisoners? Never! I'll make you dance in the air instead!" He closed one nostril, and with the other blew the two regiments of horse sky high, one man here, one there, up and over the mountains.

One good sergeant cried for mercy, and Blow eased off a little to let him come down without harm. Then he said to him: "Go back to your king and tell him to send as many horsemen as he likes; I will send them all flying."

When the king had received this message, he said:
"Let them go, the rascals. They have won."

So the six companions took home their treasure, divided it among themselves, and lived happily ever after.